THE COMPASSION

A TALE TO AWAKEN HOPE AND JOY WITHIN US

DEBANJAN ROY

Dedicated to the sacred memory of my Baba (Father) Late
Debi Prosad Roy, and Maa (Mother) Late Shubhra Roy.

None of them is now on this earth in their physical forms.
But I have the strongest faith that both of them are always
with me and guiding me at every moment of my life.

So, it is an honour to submit my offering at their lotus feet
and seek their blessings.

Debanjan

Contents

Homage

To make this book possible, I am ever grateful to my Guru, Her Holiness (late) Sri Archana Puri Maa of Sree Satyananda Devayatan, Kolkata.

Her Holiness had Graced my life through the sacred 'Mantra Deeksha' (Spiritual Initiation) in 2006.

Her blessings have been the continual source of my inspiration ever since I took up the pen and began writing.

Pranam at the lotus feet of my Guru!

Debanjan

An Earnest Appeal

My Brothers and Sisters,

You are the beloved people for whom this book is meant. This compendium is meant to reignite hope and joy in your life, in whatever little way it can.

Through my own painful experience, I've come to realize that, so many of us are silently carrying bleeding wounds in our hearts all the time. Our tears, our pain, and our wounds inside our hearts may not always be visible under the veneer of our smiling faces.

But, let us not surrender completely to dejection - God is there watching over us, though it may not always be apparent to us, under the weight of our anguish.

Have faith in God, who has sent each one of us to this earth with some definite mission and is watching over us always.

Remember, God is guiding us all the time so that we may fulfil that Divine mission, despite whatever ups and downs we may have suffered in this life so far.

Plus, do remember that everything on this mortal plane is temporary - nothing ever lasts - so our pain will surely lessen in intensity over a period of time, albeit gradually.

Thus, at the end of this long road, we shall become healed, whole and joyful once again: it is our God-given right.

And should you wish to share your anguish in your heart with me and thus, unburden yourself even one tiny bit, you are most welcome to do so.

With Love and Compassion,

Debanjan

debanjan73.roy@gmail.com

Prayers Of Commencement

Dear God,

    I consider You as our Divine Mother, Maa.

    Maa, Please bless us.

    And always guide each one of us on the righteous path.

    Bowing down to You,

    Debanjan

CHAPTER I

Central Theme

God has created all of us and all are equal in Divine eyes.

This implies when we are serving others, we are serving God.

Now, there are many who are less fortunate than us in life. So let us spare a thought and have "compassion" for them in whatever way we can.

After all, each one of us walks this earth for a short while indeed.

Let the memorable words of Dr Albert Schweitzer, one of the luminaries of the modern age, be our beacon at all times: *'The purpose of human life is to serve, to show compassion and the will to help others.'*

CHAPTER II

The Beginning

<u>Some words of solace:</u>
  Be the reason someone smiles.
  - Roy J Bennet

<u>*The Story Unfolds...*</u>

Ganesh and his friends (Rakesh, Ashok and Devesh) have passed out from a reputed Engineering College in West Bengal and then joined a Fortune 500 I.T firm in Noida in Uttar Pradesh as Trainees. Two of them, Ganesh and Rakesh, hailing from Kolkata, are temporarily lodged in a hostel in Delhi.

Here, the warden - cum - canteen in charge is a South Indian gentleman, Shri A.V. Rao, nicknamed Sir ji. He has been in this post for the last two decades and is an institution by himself.

The narrative opens through the emotions surging through Ganesh as he sits moved by chance contact with the human misery on the street.

Come, let us join him now...

Ganesh was silently sitting at the canteen table - a steaming cup of coffee was getting cold - a plate of just fried 'vada' (vegetable fritter) was meeting the same fate too. It was around 5 PM on a lazy Saturday evening. And the date was September 4, 2021. The peak of the corona scare had subsided and life was reverting to normal everywhere.

It was a weekend off for Ganesh - he was now working in Infocomm India Ltd., one of the reputed Fortune 500

I.T. MNCs. Normally this was a time when Ganesh was in a jovial mood but today seemed to be an exception. Something was tugging at him from the inside – as a result, he was not in a mood to enjoy his simple but delicious tiffin.

The canteen had been almost empty so far. Now it saw the entry of Rakesh, the childhood friend of Ganesh: both of them had grown up together in a decent locality of South Kolkata, been educated at the same missionary school in Kolkata and graduated from the reputed institution of the National Institute of Technology, Durgapur.

Now both of them had been working in Infocom India since July 2021: they had joined this Organization as Graduate Engineer Trainees (GET) through campus selection amidst tough competition.

Since both of them belonged to Kolkata and Infocomm had posted them at its India Head Quarters in Noida, they had taken temporary accommodation in a working men's hostel in Lajpat Nagar, Delhi. Company transport picked them up in the morning to Noida and then dropped them at their hostel in the evening.

Now, Ganesh was tall and lanky, with a serious face topped by a crown of straight black hairs, parted on the right like a school student - he was not much into the fashion of clothing or hairstyle. A simple cotton shirt and trousers were his everyday wear, be it in his office, his hostel, or at weekend trips to malls and movies.

Hailing from a middle-class family of a long line of professors, doctors and lawyers, he had been brought up strictly. For him, the values he had imbibed from his Granny since his childhood were sacrosanct.

He always cherished her daily reading of scriptures such as 'Gita', after the evening 'Arati' at the shrine at home. And the stories he picked up from her readings of the great epics such as 'Ramayana' and 'Mahabharata' remain fresh in his mind to this day.

She had received the sacred 'Deeksha' at the holy premise of Ramakrishna Math, Belur (near Kolkata) in 1985. And in April 2019, Ganesh followed in her footstep too when he heeded the call of his heart and received his sacred 'Deeksha' at the same holy place. Though the parents were not too pleased by this deed of their only son, his Granny was quite happy about it.

Rakesh, the bosom friend of Ganesh complemented the latter nicely as he was almost opposite in nature. Dusky and well-toned through regular exercising in the gym, he belonged to an affluent business family in Kolkata that had trading interests in tea and jute.

He was of a medium height with a face that broke into a radiant smile often - this one single virtue made him popular for his smile was always spreading the sunshine of joy all around.

Like a true-blooded Bengali, his passion was football. In Kolkata, he had been an active supporter of East Bengal Club and the European Premiere League matches always kept him glued to the TV in his spare time. He knew almost every minor detail of Premier League players - he himself was a good footballer.

He had a keen sense of grooming as per the latest fashion: his arrival was always preceded by the aroma of expensive perfume he used. While Ganesh was reticent by his very nature, Rakesh was an out-and-out extrovert. Just as they say that opposites attract, those two had been best friends since childhood. Now they were working in the same Company.

'What's the matter with Ganesh?' inwardly mused Rakesh, 'Why does he look so gloomy today?'

Points to Ponder:-

- *Each of us will be provided with the opportunity at some turn of our day-to-day life to do a little act of goodness for others.*
- *Let's make full use of such opportunities for showing kindness to others.*
- *Both the giver and receiver of such little touches of humanity get blessed in life.*

CHAPTER III

A Tale of Empathy

<u>*Some words of solace:*</u>
The words of kindness are more healing to a drooping heart than balm or honey.
- Sarah Fielding

The venue of the meeting between the two buddies was the canteen, an oblong and fairly wide room that almost covered the length of an entire wing of the hostel. And keeping with the time-honoured tradition in any government-run establishment, the canteen in particular and the hostel building in general seldom saw any painting or other forms of maintenance.

The coat of paint on the canteen walls was peeling here and there: the last painting job had been carried out ages ago and since then, those walls had come to acquire an indeterminate greyish colour. Only close scrutiny by an interested observer would have revealed its original blue tint. These walls must have looked bright when freshly painted, but now they gave, at best, indifferent looks at the legions of hungry men who crowded the canteen in the morning, noon and night.

For furniture, the room boasted of six circular tables of ancient vintage, with equally ancient four chairs per table. While this eating establishment's primary task was serving meals to the hostel inmates, it also sold coffee and snacks to outsiders at tiffin time.

In one corner, the serving counter was there, at whose head sat an impressively proportioned man, Shri A V Rao, called Sir ji by everyone around. Sir ji, hailing from

Hyderabad, had landed in Delhi in search of livelihood decades ago. After trying his hand at several odd jobs here and there, he finally landed the cushy job of hostel warden - cum - canteen in charge.

In the canteen, there were two waiters to take orders and one boy to take care of the housekeeping. The cook, 'Bhola ji', another old hand and with equally ample bodily proportions, reigned supreme in the kitchen in all his glory. While both Sir ji and Bhola ji had been blessed with an amiable disposition, the former had the additional quality of a booming voice. Together they were the de facto boss in the hostel: the working men staying there meekly surrendered to their sway.

Now, as Rakesh came in unobtrusively and drew up a chair to sit, Ganesh chose to remain silent - his gaze was lost somewhere in the monsoon sky beyond the canteen windows. Suddenly Rakesh was startled to note two silent teardrops glistening at the corner of his friend's eyes. He could no longer resist breaking the oppressive silence, and blurted out, 'Buddy, what's the matter?'

While he had been long accustomed to the habitually thoughtful silence of his friend, the tears he saw today were a surprise indeed! So, in a tone of concern, he repeated his query. Even then Ganesh did not respond immediately - the verdant greenery of the Neem tree visible through the canteen windows seemed to attract him more.

But on being prodded for the third time by his now visibly impatient friend, Ganesh whispered in a tone, rendered almost inaudible due to tears, 'Why is life so unfair?'

Rakesh, straining his ears to catch the soft and husky words of Ganesh, was simply dumbfounded at this unexpected googly. At his 21 years of peak youth, he had never encountered such a profound question till now - he was thus frankly at a loss how to reply.

His uneasy silence made Ganesh repeat his philosophical question. This time, however, Rakesh's naturally friendly nature kicked in and he responded in a voice full of friendly empathy, ' Buddy, will you tell me everything in detail?' When Ganesh hesitated, he persisted like a bulldog. 'Come on Ganesh,' pleaded Rakesh, 'just begin from the beginning. For heaven's sake, out with it, man!'

In the meanwhile, Rakesh beckoned to a waiter-boy to get the cup and plates of now-cold coffee and 'vada' removed and get them fresh ones: in sign language, he indicated to Sir ji that he would foot the bill. And the ever-prudent Sir ji, already familiar with the habits of his hostel - inmates, compiled promptly - within a short time, he sent over two plates of freshly fried 'vada' to them, along with two tumblers of coffee to wash the food down.

At Rakesh's insistence, Ganesh gingerly took a sip of the nicely brewed coffee - this was one tiffin item, that was truly good at the canteen. And then responding to the affectionate body language of his buddy, Ganesh began confiding in a sombre tone: 'It all started at the Lajpat Nagar Market complex today morning - I had gone to Agrawal Mobile Store there to get a new memory card for my mobile phone. As you know, I have to regularly download documents for my induction project report and keeping them on my mobile is far handier than on my laptop.'

'Yes, I know', Rakesh nodded in agreement, 'I too need to brush up on that report. It's a good thing that you reminded me about.' Both of them knew what a stickler for deadlines their Team Lead, Mahesh Sir was and within a month of their joining, they had already witnessed what a ruckus he could create in case of any delay in completion of an agreed assignment!

'Yeah, that's why I went to buy that memory card,' confided Ganesh in an unusual bout of talkative mood, 'it cost me a bit more than I thought. It was while I was making payment to Agarwal ji, the shop-proprietor via Paytm that he casually happened to make a mention of the latest model of iPhone that had just arrived in his shop - I simply gave an involuntary shiver when I heard its price tag!'

'Buddy, as you know, the long-standing credo of our family has always been: 'simple living and high thinking.' So, I politely declined Agrawal ji's offer to show me that iPhone - for me, my present mobile was good enough. And simultaneously I also noted the extent to which the pernicious consumerism of the 21st Century is impacting us at all levels - we are being constantly encouraged to buy a new consumer product even when its existing counterpart at our home is still good enough to last for several years more!'

In a mood of self-reflection, Ganesh resumed, after taking a small bite of the crispy 'vada' - the taste was delicious! It is worth mentioning that all South Indian tiffin items of this Canteen carried a good reputation as Bhola ji was an expert cook indeed. 'With mixed thoughts about iPhones and other costly yet needless luxury items, I came out of the shop. And then I saw.'

Saying this Ganesh stopped tantalizingly in mid-sentence, which prompted the curious Rakesh to query ' And you saw what?' 'As I stepped onto the footpath to reach my parked scooty,' replied Ganesh, 'I came across two children, a girl and a boy standing side by side and begging on the road. From their face, they seemed to belong to a decent background, yet they were dressed shabbily in ill-fitting clothes. They must have taken recourse to beg only recently, as they seemed to be quite ashamed in approaching anyone for alms.'

'Both of them seemed hardly 10-12 years of age,' continued Ganesh, 'and bore a striking facial resemblance to each other. Quite possibly they were siblings, with the girl seemingly slightly older of the two. Before they had to undergo the shame of stretching their hands, I took a fifty rupee note out of my purse. Then I mechanically handed over that note to the small palm of the girl, with half of my mind busy thinking about the quickest route from the shop to my hostel.'

'But, then, something in their innocent demeanour, not matching that of usual street beggars, arrested my attention. Prodded by some unknown instinct, I came closer to them and asked the girl as gently as I could: 'Dear child, why are two of you standing here and begging? Where is the Mummy-Papa of both of you?' Initially, they were quite scared to confide in me, but after a while, the little girl picked up the courage to reply in a very soft and pain-stricken voice, 'Bhaiya, now both of them are no more'.

'Shocked to the core, I then ventured to ask them (who looked famished), if they had eaten anything since morning - it was just an instinctive urge of kindness that arose within me at that moment. Due to their natural shyness, they were reluctant to reply any further to a complete stranger. But then, probably, the silent wave of concern emanating from my heart, coupled with pangs of hunger overcame their hesitation and the small boy admitted in a feeble voice that they had not.'

'Hearing this, I straight away went to the nearest grocery store and purchased a big loaf of bread, along with two pouches each of jam and flavoured milk. Coming back, I offered the foodstuff to the children silently - after much hesitation, they accepted my humble offering and sat down on the footpath itself to eat. My goodness! How hungrily they gulped down their food!'

'Seeing them eat filled me up with an inner glow of joy - truly, nothing ever can come close to small acts of generosity in creating authentic happiness for us. And our lives are filled with such opportunities every day - all we have to do is to take notice and act on them immediately.'

Points to Ponder:

- *Almost every one of us is nursing our wounds in our hearts and only we know how much it pains.*
- *Let us do our bit to lessen that pain: just quietly listening to the outpouring of an anguished soul will work wonders.*
- *All it takes is a little bit of willingness.*

CHAPTER IV

A Saga of Human Selfishness

<u>Some words of solace:</u>

Our prime purpose in this life is to help others. And, if you can't help them, at least don't hurt them.

- Dalai Lama XIV

Ganesh in a voice charged with positivity resumed, 'I waited on my scooty as the children finished their simple meal with gusto. Then I asked them gently, 'If you want anything more, just tell me. Don't be shy - after all, you have called me your brother.'

'Now something in my loving tone must have touched their innocent heart as in response both of them dissolved in a flood of tears. I waited for them to regain their composure and looked the other way, as passersby continuously gave us curious looks.'

'As the children quietened down, I suggested 'Come, the park is ahead - let's go there.' This time they heeded my gentle suggestion without any prompting and accompanied me to the municipal park adjacent to the market square. All three of us sat down on an empty bench and then in fits and starts, amidst some more tears, I came to know about the full extent of their tragedy.'

'Their names were Neetu and Sanju: they belonged to Meerut, where their father was working as a grocery shopkeeper. Though not well-off, their parents had high hopes of them and placed them in 'Saraswati Shishu Mandir', a really good school there. However, in a shocking turn of events, they had lost both their parents, one after another, over the last six months due to the recent outbreak of Corona.'

'A helpful Delhi-based N.G.O had taken the children away in the nick of the time and put them in an isolated ward in a clinic in Delhi; else they could have met the same fate too. Later on, this N.G.O contacted their 'Mama' in Agra, on their behalf - he kindly consented to take the custody of his orphaned nephew and niece.'

'But their cruel destiny had stored more pains for them. In the company of their Mama, the sorrowful children went to his house in Agra. And, they soon discovered his wife was an absolute despot - under no circumstances, she was going to allow their unwelcome burden (the way she saw it) to eat into the meagre earning of the household. Their Mama was a petty accountant with a local 'Seth ji' and he already had two daughters of his own.'

'For several months, the children tried their best to adjust. Their Mama, who was a decent person by nature, also kept up his efforts to convince his wife that their nephew and niece could be put into some free government school and that their expenses would not amount to much. After all, the Central Government had already declared eligibility of a child - orphaned due to the Corona outbreak - to receive a stipend every month. But alas! She was adamant - in her view, the paltry Government stipend would be insufficient to cover their expenses in these inflationary times.'

'Shockingly, taking a cue from their mother, their cousins also began misbehaving with them. They were constantly made to carry out all sorts of menial tasks - their lot was no better than that of a servant. But having no other alternative, they had to meekly comply with every unjust demand made on them such as fetching buckets of water, scrubbing the floor of the house, and washing the utensils.

Such tasks should never have been given to them as their bodies were frail with malnutrition.

'The elder girl had somehow been tolerating every form of torture for the sake of her younger brother. But one particular day, the proverbial straw broke the camel's back: she discovered her Mami badly beating her beloved 'Bhai' with a stick. Something snapped within her as she witnessed this gross abuse: she rushed forward, snatched the stick away from Mami's hand and pushed her down in anger. And firmly holding the hands of her brother, she made an instant decision to run away. It was not a very wise decision but then tolerance of abuse has got its limit, even for children.'

'It is well said that God helps those, who help themselves. Both the children had been blessed in one sense: right from their earliest days, they had witnessed their pious mother worshipping daily at the little shrine they had in their cramped two-room house back in Meerut. They, too, had subconsciously imbibed this righteous habit of praying to God every day. Even during their abuse-laden stay at their Mama's home at Agra, they had kept up this noble practice in the silence of their minds.'

'Now, as they ran from their Mama's house, they kept on praying to God to show them the way. And, sure enough, a friendly cyclist turned up and directed them to the market complex where their Mama worked. After reaching there, the children began asking the shopkeepers for the garment store where their Mama worked as an accountant and finally, a young lad, working in a stationery shop nearby, took them to that store.'

'They found their Mama inside, with a visibly worried look - he had already been alerted by his wife, over mobile, about the running away of his niece and nephew. And a single look at their tear-stained faces, carrying signs of physical abuse, was enough to tell Mama everything that must have happened in his house. Feeling profusely sorry, he awkwardly confessed to the children that the only option left to them was to go back to the Delhi-based N.G.O which had initially cared for them after the death of their parents. Else, they would meet similar abuse at the houses of other relatives as well - these were the same relatives who were so well behaved when their parents were alive but would now show a completely different face altogether.'

'So, he called up the in-charge of the N.G.O and explained everything to her - in the end, he requested her to take back the custody of his orphaned niece and nephew. He kept the outcome of the conversation to himself. Thereafter, he took the children to Agra Railway Station, bought them two tickets to Delhi, and gave them thousand rupees in cash (for which his wife was sure to give him a hard time later on) along with the contact details and directions to reach the office of N.G.O in Nizamuddin, Delhi. Finally, he got them seated in a second-class compartment of a Delhi bound train and bade them goodbye.'

'The lonely and scared children got down at the Nizamuddin Railway Station, and as advised by Mama, they walked to the nearby office of the N.G.O. There more shock lay in store for them as this N.G.O flatly refused them admission as they were already overburdened with so many other orphans and didn't have more room. They had already conveyed this decision over the phone to their Mama, who had kept it to himself. So, they were referred to another homeless children's shelter in nearby Lajpat Nagar.'

'For the last week or so, they had been putting up at this shelter named 'Ashiana'. But as their cruel fate would have it, the shelter was cash-strapped: so, while they had a roof over their head, their meals were very irregular. With the little money given by their Mama being already spent on buying food during this past week, they had reached the point of starvation.'

'So out of desperation, they had decided to try and seek alms at the local market complex since yesterday morning. Today was their second day of a try at the begging but their inner sense of shame made it into a very difficult proposition. This was their condition when I met them today morning.' - concluded a visibly upset Ganesh.

'One thing that deeply pains me,' Ganesh remarked in a mood of self-reflection a little while later, 'Why can't we use a bit of more kindness in our speech during our day-to-day lives? After all, it does not cost a single paisa to speak a few gentle words to a soul in distress. It will save us from so much of the needless pain that we keep on casually inflicting upon one another.' Saying this, he came to a full stop.

Points to ponder:

- *We should be very careful of our tongue because even a single harsh word can hurt deeply.*
- *We ourselves, at some point in our life, must have been at the receiving end of sharp verbal arrows; so, we know the terrible pain of their sting very well.*
- *So, let's always consciously cultivate the virtue of being kind to others in our speech.*

CHAPTER V

A Clash of Perspectives

<u>*Some words of solace:*</u>
There is more happiness in giving than in receiving.
- Acts 20:35
There is no greater loan than a sympathetic ear.
- Frank Tyger

Rakesh had remained quiet all through the lengthy narration. His companionable silence prompted Ganesh to add, 'Here on one hand we have people willing to merrily spend Rs.60,000 - Rs.70,000 on a luxury item such as an iPhone that they probably don't even need, while at the same time we have little children on the streets who do not have even Rs.100 with them to spend on food and other bare essentials of life - this life is just so unfair!'

Overcome with a mixture of empathy, remorse and helplessness, Ganesh was unable to continue anymore - he just laid down his face on the table and broke down in tears. He was a very sensitive soul indeed!

Now, Rakesh, being much more worldly-wise and possessing a different framework of looking at things, did not intervene immediately. Wisely he decided to allow Ganesh sufficient time and space to collect himself.

Sure enough, after a longish interval, Ganesh sat up on his own. However, he made no attempt to wipe away his tears, remaining oblivious to the stares of Sir ji, the canteen boys and Bhola ji, peeping from behind the kitchen door. And by a quirk of fate, the canteen was empty save for these two customers - this was quite an unusual occurrence on a weekend evening. Both men sat still for quite some time -

none wanted to come out from the pall of silence - it was as though they were instinctively realizing the essence of the proverb, 'If speech is silver then silence is golden.'

After a while, the sound of approaching footsteps could be heard - soon two more young men, Devesh and Ashok walked in and joined the duo at the table. They were all classmates from the same College. And they loved to spend their weekend evenings together.

Ashok, belonging to the city of Gurgaon, had received his schooling in Delhi and gone on to join NIT - Durgapur. He was a fairly tall fellow with 5'10" height, who was passionate about a rarity these days: Hindustani Classical Music - he was quite a good singer himself, having received training in vocal music under the renowned 'Patiala Gharana' for a decade or so.

And Devesh, hailing from the walled city of Old Delhi, was equally tall and well-built to boot. He was an avid cricketer, who had the good fortune of being part of his school as well as NIT -Durgapur's cricket teams. And like the pair of Ganesh and Rakesh, these two men had opposite temperaments: Devesh was outgoing while Ashok was comparatively reserved.

The newcomers could make out that something serious was afoot from the grave facial expression of their friends. At their request, Rakesh briefed them about the gist of the matter while Ganesh continued to sit somberly. To lighten the gloomy atmosphere, Rakesh asked them what they would like to eat. On being informed that they had a late Saturday lunch, he exclaimed, 'Come on, buddy! Have a cup of coffee at least - it will serve as a nice post-meal dessert.'

And without waiting to hear any more objection, he simply beckoned Sir ji to send them two cups of filter coffee, the speciality of the canteen. As they waited for the coffee to arrive, Devesh asked in a low tone, 'Ganesh, what are you thinking so deeply about? Won't you like to share with us?'

Ganesh replied equally softly, 'Buddy! I am getting constant recollections of Neetu and Sanju. After finishing our conversation, all three of us came out of the park: I proceeded to my scooty while the children took the road to 'Ashiana', the homeless children's shelter. I again gave them a fifty rupee note but giving such alms is just a stop-gap measure. I want to help them on a long-term basis but simply don't know what I should do - all I know is I want to do something for them - after all, those two kids have called me 'Bhaiya' (elder brother).'

'So, it effectively means that if all and sundry beggars on the road address you as 'Bhaiya', you will melt immediately and start doing out your hard-earned cash to them?' questioned Rakesh in a mildly challenging tone, 'Do you think that money grows on trees in your park? How do you know for sure that those begging children did not take you for a ride? They could have so easily cooked up a cock and bull story to get free lunch and a gift of hundred rupees to boot from a naive stranger like you. You are so gullible, man! Anyone can tell you a fabricated story to extract money from you. Boss, when are you going to learn at least a little bit of worldliness?'

Ashok, who had been silently listening to their exchange, now spoke up in favour of Ganesh, 'I think Amar Colony is not far from this hostel: one of us can easily go to 'Ashiana' and verify the antecedents of those children. Alternatively, we can trace the phone number of 'Ashiana' from 'just dial' and make necessary enquiries. Plus, spending a little on buying food for a child beggar is no big deal - the same goes for giving away alms of hundred rupees to him. Don't forget that the amount we spend every week on our uber cab rides alone will be many times this partly sum.'

This short but succinct rejoinder by Ashok raised hackles in Rakesh even more. He could not bear even the thought of spending one's hard-earned money just for the sake of charity alone - in his merchant family, he had witnessed how even charity was an indirect arm of the business. 'Ashok, so you mean to say,' Rakesh remarked in an aggressive voice, 'Ganesh will start bearing the burden of day-to-day living expenses of any random beggar he comes across on the street?'

When neither Ganesh nor Ashok chose to respond, a merciless Rakesh continued his attack, 'Has Ganesh taken up the contract to look after beggar-children? Is he going to throw away the money he is rightfully earning through ten to twelve hours of daily toil at Infocomm on such senseless charity?'

Being a worldly-wise person, Rakesh considered his duty lay in bringing his 'goody-goody' friends to their senses. From his standpoint of pure practicality, Ganesh had already acted in a childishly naive manner by frittering away money in feeding and giving alms to beggars. Now, by wanting to do something even more for them in future, Ganesh was guilty of an even bigger sin in his worldly eyes. It was the unpardonable sin of indulging in something as impractical and futile as 'philanthropy'. It was clear that a classic standoff was at hand between two dramatically opposite perspectives on life.

In the meanwhile, Ashok had succeeded in tracing the contact details of Ashiana and after making necessary enquiries, he announced to the group that two children named Neetu and Sanju were indeed staying there. Rakesh was quite nonplussed to find that his suspicion about the two children was misplaced.

Points to Ponder:

- *Most of us have been blessed by God with a steady means of income.*
- *So, come, besides spending the bulk of that income on ourselves and our families, let us spend a tiny fraction on charity also.*
- *It is we who will get blessed by even little acts of generosity. Remember no good deed ever goes in vain.*

CHAPTER VI

A Road Less Travelled

Ganesh, true to his spiritual grounding, remained composed while taking his own sweet time in framing his reply. He always tried to avoid giving knee-jerk reactions to any challenge thrown at him by the incessant demands of daily life.

Being a voracious reader, he had come across a valuable piece of advice in 'Udbodhan', the reputed monthly journal of Ramakrishna Mission.

This advice was given by Swami Premeshananda ji: the revered Swami had emphasised that one of the clearest indicators of spiritual progress in life is our ability to remain calm in trying situations with the corresponding ability to regain our composure quickly if we do happen to get agitated in such a situation.

He found that the time had now arrived to put this valuable learning into practice by calmly considering the viewpoints of Rakesh on merits. And as he did so, he found that a forked road faced him: - either he could give in to Rakesh's opinion, or he could stick to his own humanitarian convictions. He chose the second option, the 'road less travelled.'

However, it needs to be stated that he found much merit in the no-nonsense judgment of Rakesh. He knew pretty well that there was no security at Infocomm: every year, it mercilessly showed doors to at least a quarter of its bench-strength of trainees for failing to meet its exacting performance standards.

And for the ones who were retained, their confirmation and salary increase took place only after a year of their joining. So, during the training period, a prudent trainee aspiring to build his savings needed to prune his expenses as much as he could. This would straightaway rule out any form of sustained philanthropy by Ganesh at this point in time. After all, he had got his financial obligations back at home.

But (and this was a crucial 'but'), he was built of different mettle - he had consistently rebelled against the path of conventional wisdom, imposed on every middle-class boy here in India. This typical norm dictated that such a boy should study hard in school to beat everyone else in marks in class Xth and XIIth Board examinations, then crack the joint entrance examinations (J.E.E) to land a coveted seat in a reputed Engineering College, then again study hard there to beat the competition to secure the highest Grade-Point Average (G.P.A), and finally, cross the hurdle of campus selection to gain a prized job in some Fortune 500 MNC.

And of course, even after getting that job, one was expected to display the same zeal in advancing in the career rat race too. In the whole chain, there would be no scope for any frivolous thing such as thinking for the needy or doing something for the underprivileged. The objective of such a ruthlessly competitive mode of living was the magic jackpot of 'a well-settled life'.

It is worth mentioning that any deviation from the conventional path is deeply frowned upon by Indian society. Examples of such deviations could be opting to do M.Tech after B.Tech (which effectively meant being out of the job market for almost two years) or opting to join a start-up after B.Tech (which would straight away imply foregoing the pay package of a cushy job in an MNC).

Ganesh, to his great credit, had always stood up against the oppressive pressures of society, as outlined above. And the lessons he had picked up in childhood while listening to his Granny's discourses from Scriptures and Epics provided ammunition for such rebellion. The biggest of such lessons in humanity was imbibed by him from his role model, Swami Vivekananda.

Under the noble influence of this Iconic Saint of Modern India, he had started doing little acts of charity during his school life. Examples of such deeds were donating blood in the camps of the Rotary Club, giving away textbooks from his previous years to needy juniors in school, freely sharing his lunch with his classmates every day and so on. Needless to add, none of this used to meet with the approval of his parents but his Granny used to always get pleased.

Later on, during his studies in college, he would invite even greater censure from his parents. This happened when they came to know that, instead of devoting time for career-enhancing pursuits such as preparation for C.A.T (Common Admission Test for IIM), he was 'wasting' his valuable time on giving free coaching in Maths to the children of slum-dwellers. To add fuel to their ire, he also used to regularly join the missionary activities of Ramakrishna Mission (such as flood relief etc.) as a student volunteer.

And he always dreamed of doing something for the underprivileged - opening a free J.E.E coaching school for deserving students with poor backgrounds was one such cherished dream. To make that dream possible, he was ready to sacrifice his corporate career, knowing fully well that his parents would oppose it tooth and nail.

The chief inspiration behind this dream was a life-changing experience he had during the third year (Vth Semester) of his college. Then he had the good fortune to personally witness a miraculous success brought about by the mighty powers of education. It had so happened that a class X boy, a son of a ragpicker living in the slum, used to be coached by him in Maths - this boy had subsequently gone on to crack the IIT entrance exams. This was a feat that even he could not accomplish despite the best of his schooling and coaching resources.

And to his credit, the success of his ward had given him even greater satisfaction than what he would have felt if he had done it himself. So, this was the real Ganesh, who now prepared to face his friend-cum-critic, Rakesh. And he knew what stand going to take.

Points to Ponder:

- *Let us mould our day-to-day lives as per the teaching of the Holy Bible: "Cast your bread upon the waters".*
- *This is a wonderful piece of advice that asks us to give generously without worrying about what we are going to get in return.*
- *And when we give unconditionally, we then forget our troubles, as an inner glow of satisfaction lights up our hearts.*

CHAPTER VII

Have Compassion for Others

<u>*Some words of solace:*</u>

I'm not a handsome guy, but I can give my hand to someone who needs help. Beauty is in the heart and not in the face.

- Dr A.P.J. Abdul Kalam

'Rakesh', said Ganesh in a thoughtful tone. 'I fully appreciate your views - it makes enormous sense from the standpoint of practicality and common sense.' Rakesh gave a smug smile in response - he felt good that his innocent friend was returning to sense at last. But his feelings of superiority lasted for a very short while when he faced a bouncer from Ganesh next moment, 'And, at the same time, it is equally important to spare a moment to think of others too.'

'Could you clarify, buddy?' queried a seemingly puzzled Rakesh. In response, Ganesh asked a counter-question, 'Rakesh, have you heard the name of Swami Vivekananda?' This time Rakesh was even more baffled but had the presence of mind to reply, 'Yes, of course. But why do you ask me now?' 'Because the answer to your first query lies in the golden words of Swami ji uttered more than a century ago: 'Let us give out of our own bounty just as God gives to us.'

'How is this saying relevant here, boss?'

'Rakesh, this inspiring message of Swamiji, my role model since childhood, is valid for all ages and is especially relevant for this ultra-materialistic 21st century. It straight away answers your query about why we should think of others also.'

'Hmm, I see.'

'And as you know well, I had taken up the vocation of giving free tuitions in Maths to slum-children while I was in NIT - it was this very call of Swamiji which had encouraged me to take that small step forward towards a greater cause.'

'Pray, what was that so-called greater cause?'

'Rakesh, that greater cause is doing at least something for our needy brethren in our society. After all, in the eyes of God, we are all equal. Yet, we now have the most unfortunate reality of tiny islands of affluence surrounded by a vast sea of poverty. And, this gulf between 'have' and 'have not' is increasing day by day - such an unenviable situation calls for immediate redressal.'

'So, is it you who has got the sole contract for redressing the societal inequalities?'

'Rakesh, the issue is not that - my individual efforts may indeed be tiny in the face of the gigantic scale of social inequality prevalent right now. But at least it is a beginning - who knows, it may be a catalyst for initiatives by many others as well. That's why I always keep in mind the clarion call of Swami ji: 'Serve Lord Shiva by serving man', which he had learnt from his Divine Guru, Bhagavan Sri Ramakrishna Dev. This ideal had formed the basis of Swami ji's exhortation to all his Indian brethren to see God in the hungry, the downtrodden, and the impoverished - I have found this ideal extremely inspiring to follow as the core value of my life.

'Ganesh, sometimes I frankly find you too naïve and impractical,' remarked Rakesh in an exasperated voice, 'from where would you get all the resources to carry out your 'goody-goody' plans? Do you think that money grows on plants? Do you believe that all you have to do is to pluck off as much cash as you desire from your favourite money plant? Just grow up man! Enough of all this impractical nonsense! Remember that this world is a much tougher place!'

'Rakesh, you seem to accuse me of being unworldly quite often these days,' responded Ganesh in a calm voice, 'but, you can never level this allegation against the success icons of our generation, Bill Gates and his wife, Melinda Gates. Gates had famously said, 'Both of us were taught to give back ... we believe all lives have an equal value and that's why we made the decision to donate our wealth from Microsoft to help others.' Currently, this couple tops the list of billionaires who are generously giving away their wealth in charity.'

'And neither can you level the same charge against one of the greatest figures in modern history - Benjamin Franklin, the writer, the scientist, the diplomat, the philosopher and one of the most revered figures as the founding father of U.S.A - by any worldly yardstick of name, fame, money or power, he is a shining example of success. But even he believed in the powers of 'goody-goody' behaviour, for every morning he would ask himself, 'What good shall I do today?' and every evening he would review, 'What good have I done today?'

'Oh! Come on, Ganesh! It is very easy to practice philanthropy when you have grown as powerful as Benjamin Franklin, or as rich as Bill Gates. But for us lesser mortals, it is far more important to earn first - only then, can we even think of charity.

'Rakesh, allow me to differ politely. Let me draw your attention to what another great icon of our modern times, President Roosevelt of USA had said - 'Do what you can, with what you have, where you are' - so each one of us, irrespective of our wealth or lack of it, can start a charity in small ways - the world will be a much better place to live then. And may I also draw your attention to what Bob Burg had advocated in his bestseller, 'Go-Giver', 'Your true worth is determined by how much more you give in value than what you receive in payment.'

'Ganesh, let others apply such esoteric ideas. Let small fry like you and I stick to the conventional mode of earning and that is 'think of own your interests first'.

'Rakesh, generosity as a means to generate wealth is not as impracticable as you claim it to be. Otherwise, hardnosed profit-seeking MNCs would never have spent so much on fulfilling their CSR, i.e., Corporate Social Responsibility. These shrewd Corporations know that 'corporate philanthropy' goes on to improve the 'corporate bottom line' too. That explains the astute remarks of Niall Fitzerald, the former CEO of Unilever Plc., 'Corporate Social Responsibility is a hard-edged business decision. Not because it is a nice thing to do, or because people are forcing us to do it ... but because it is good for our business.'

'A sound case for generosity was also made by another great business best-seller, 'The One Minute Millionaire'. It had said, 'Giving as you get acknowledges the Universe as truly abundant...The enlightened millionaire knows this: there is an ocean of abundance and one can tap into it with teaspoon/bucket/tractor-trailer - the ocean does not care.'

'So, my dear friend, generosity, i.e., thinking and caring about others is a practically tested business strategy for generating wealth.'

Points to Ponder:

* *To be successful is to be helpful.*

 - Dr Norman Vincent Peale

- *The world is round. And what you give, comes back to you. What you send out, comes back. What you sow, you reap. What you give, you get ...*

  - Unknown

- *Remember, life is an echo. It always gets back to you. So, give goodness.*

  - Unknown

- *Who achieve great things that the world will never forget, start out by accomplishing small things that the world will never see.*

  - Bob Burg

CHAPTER VIII

A Glimmer of Spiritual Insight

Some words of solace:

Small acts of kindness can make a difference in other people's lives more than we can imagine.

- Catherine Pulsifer

Even if you think you have very little to offer, it doesn't matter; it's purely the act of kindness that is important. What you may think is small or not very important, can mean everything to someone else.

- Giovanna Tucker

Ganesh and Rakesh were now locked into an ideological battle: the former was a firm proponent of compassion and charity while the latter was standing his ground as a votary of self-interest and practicality. None was ready to budge an inch.

Renewing the clash, Rakesh now declared in an emphatic tone, 'Ganesh, all the examples you have quoted just now, comprise of sayings and doings of human beings like you and me. So, these are not infallible nor do they have uniform applicability in all situations and at all times.'

'Rakesh, sorry to rebut you again.', responded Ganesh in a measured voice, 'All our holy scriptures, cutting across Religions, also speak in the similar language of compassion, generosity and selflessness. That's why, since the time I came across the two destitute children begging in the market square, I have been constantly thinking of how I can help - after all, I am now earning a handsome package and thus, I can afford to spend a tiny fraction of that amount on a noble cause.'

'Oh! What an airy-fairy way of thinking!' exploded Rakesh, 'How many beggars can you help? Do you have any idea how many beggars are there in Lajpat Nagar alone? And why do you have to help in the first place?'

'Because, Rakesh, our scriptures teach us that all living beings are identical at the fundamental level. I learnt about this fascinating insight from our sacred scripture of Gita, which my Granny reads and explains every day as part of evening worship at home. Later on, my spiritual bent of mind led me to discover that other holy scriptures such as Upanishad and Srimad Bhagavat Puran also advocate the same lofty ideal.'

'And this concept of the fundamental unity of living beings has led me to understand that when we extend our hand in support of another human being, then we are helping ourselves only. I can refer to the net and extract all the relevant 'shlokas' for you if you are interested to hear the exact wordings of our holy scriptures on this supremely important concept.'

'While I thank you for sharing such deep insights from our scriptures, I have my right to differ even then,' retorted a sprightly Rakesh, 'Assuring your understanding to be correct, where will that lead us to? The way I see it, if all human beings are considered to be a manifestation of one single reality, then our modern economy will have no leg to stand upon, as its basic tenet is 'competition'. And such ethos demand that I must look upon another human being as my competitor and hence, a different entity.'

'And without competition, all quest for human excellence stops too, leaving behind a sea of stagnation all around. For example, both of us are competing with each other to advance in our respective careers towards better designations, more work responsibilities and ultimately, greater monetary rewards. Will this upward pursuit ever happen in the absence of competition? Will this continual betterment ever happen if we start thinking in terms of sharing our wealth in charity, instead of competing for earning more wealth? So, pardon me: I simply don't buy all your goody-goody philosophy.'

Devesh and Ashok had remained silent so far. But despite his usual reticence, something made Ashok feel compelled to speak up now: 'Stop! I say. Just stop!' he exclaimed, 'Here is Ganesh whose large-heartedness has made him empathise with two destitute children, who have been dealt hard blows by the cruel hand of destiny. All he has done so far is shed some tears and spend a paltry sum on feeding them just once.'

'Yet, Rakesh, you have been continuously bashing him as if he has already spent extravagantly on them! Chill down for heaven's sake!' After blurting out this long sentence in one go, he paused to catch his breath.

In a few moments, he resumed his monologue, but in a more conciliatory tone this time: 'If you ask me, I am truly proud of Ganesh for at least thinking about the underprivileged of our society. That means he has successfully managed to withstand the pernicious brainwashing by our 'higher education' system, which teaches us to think only about climbing up the career ladder and amassing money. It is so refreshing to find that the virtues like empathy and compassion, so rare in this greedy 21st-century society, are still present in him. And to me, that is what which counts the most.'

As Ashok concluded this rare bout of verbal eloquence, he found his three friends looking at him with appreciation tinged with mild incredulity - such a passionate speech was so unusual of him! And while the initial impulse of the fighting spirit of Rakesh was to verbally challenge Ashok point-by-point, saner counsel seemed to prevail: - he changed his mind and opted, instead, in favour of 'golden silence'. Everyone felt that they had enough of argumentation and an uneasy calm descended on their table. Soon a waiter-boy discreetly set four cups of steaming filter coffee before them and the four friends began to sip this refreshing drink in grateful silence.

Points to ponder:

- *A devotee always sees himself in all beings and all beings in himself because he knows that it is God who has acquired all the forms.*

    -Gita, Chapter 29, Shloka 6

- *He who sees everything in Self and Self in everything, comes to refrain from looking at anyone with hatred.*

    -Ishopanishad, Shloka 6

- *A Yogi sees all beings within Self because the Self is the point of origin of all beings - he sees Self within all beings because Self is also the point of dissolution of all beings. (Srimad Bhagavat Puran, Skanda 3, Shloka 28)*

CHAPTER IX

Memento Mori

<u>*Some words of solace:*</u>

People you love never die. That is what Omai had said all those years ago. And he was right. They don't die. Not completely. They live in your mind, the way they always lived inside you. You keep their light alive. If you remember them well enough, they can still guide you, like the shine of long-extinguished stars could guide ships in unfamiliar waters.

- Matt Haig

The pall of silence at the table of four friends was almost imperceptibly made to vanish by the mellow tone of Sir ji - 'Hello guys! How's the coffee?' One of his great virtues was his uncanny ability to sense tension at any of the tables at his canteen and then diffuse it quickly with the timely serving of snacks and coffee.

Long ago, he had learnt from his grandmother that the way to a man's heart lay through his stomach: subsequently, he found this idea to have evergreen applicability at his canteen. That's because it is very difficult for a canteen patron to relish the smell and taste of a delicious 'vada' and remain annoyed at the same time.

Rakesh, ever ready to speak up and take the lead, responded on behalf of the whole group. 'Sir ji - the coffee is really good.' He continued in a genuinely pleased voice, 'And thanks a lot for bringing us this delightful refreshment in the midst of our heated arguments.' 'Guys, you are most welcome', responded the ever-amiable Sir ji - this was the opening he was looking out for to join the group.

On his discreet signal, a waiter boy immediately fetched him a chair to sit, much to the joy of the assembled group. And that was because Sir ji carried a reputation of being a good conversationalist.

'Hope you guys do not mind my joining you,' remarked Sir ji as he sat down, 'and I hope I am not interrupting your coffee break'. 'Of course, not! you are most welcome' responded Ganesh hastily.

'In that case,' suggested Sir ji, 'let us all move to my office. We shall have privacy as I have something very important to share with you.'

The group finished their coffee and then left the canteen together to proceed to the adjoining office of Sir ji. Here the furniture was much superior to that in the canteen. As everybody comfortably settled themselves in the three-piece sofa in the room, Sir ji spoke up.

'For the last half an hour or so, I have been a silent spectator of your group. And I could not help overhearing most of your talks, as the whole canteen was empty, save for you guys. So, as your senior and well-wisher, you will please pardon me, if I take the liberty of asking a few very personal questions now.'

His young audience, not being sure of what was there in his mind, simply nodded.

Thus emboldened, Sir ji queried, 'Tell me, why are you guys slogging so hard now?'

As the four young men took time to digest this unexpected inquiry, they mentally conceded the point of Sir ji: on average, 9 to 10 hours were being put in by them every working day at Infocomm. On some days, their working day stretched to 12 hours...on top of that, sometimes they had to bring work home also!

'Well, that's because we want to progress fast in our career.' replied Rakesh, the de facto leader.

'How will that help you?'

'Fast career progression will help us climb the corporate ladder fast - that will help us to earn a ton of money and enjoy life.'

'And how long will that enjoyment last?'

This grenade made the whole group puzzled: they did not know what had come over Sir ji all of a sudden.

Sir ji was normally found enthusiastically discussing Cricket with the young men of the hostel. He used to sound so animated then! But today he seemed to be in a completely different mood altogether.

He seemed to be bent on poking them with one provocative question after another. 'Why is he doing this?' wondered each of the young men. An uncomfortable silence enveloped all four.

Ganesh, the ever-intuitive guy spoke up in an unsure tone to break the silence, 'Sir ji, I'm not too sure of what you exactly want to know. The only thing I can venture from my knowledge of the scriptures is that enjoyment of earthly pleasures can't go on forever. It has to end at some point in time in future.'

'Do you know when?'

'Oh! Come on Sir ji! Why are you raising such uncomfortable questions now? All four of us here are hardly 21-22 years of age; the whole life lies stretched in front of us for enjoying ourselves to the full.' - pat came the self-assured reply of Rakesh.

'No buddy,' Ganesh softly intervened. 'You cannot be so certain. Just look at the case of our classmate Sushil, whose elder brother expired in his own office chamber at the age of 40 last week - was it the age for him to go?'

The news of this tragedy had reached them just two days ago: the cause of death was said to be a sudden cardiac arrest.

'Oh, that was an exception buddy,' pitched in a confident Devesh, 'not everyone is destined to pass away at an early age. And as Rakesh rightly says, all four of us have a lo ... o...ng time to live and enjoy life – after all, we are in the prime of our youth now.'

'Are you so sure?' came the mystifying response of Sir ji; he was not going to let them off the hook so easily.

Hearing this, a baffled Ashok pleaded, 'Sir ji, could you come clean, please? Do tell us what is on your mind - don't keep us in suspense any longer.'

In response, Sir ji chose to take a significant pause and remain quiet for a while, lost in his reflection. Now the four pals were sure that something was gnawing at his heart.

And, their guess was proved right when in an eerie repetition of what had happened just an hour ago with Ganesh, the normally jovial face of Sir ji gradually crumpled into silent tears. It was a stunning shock as he was quite a boisterous man at normal times!

However, Ganesh, blessed with an innate sense of empathy, was the first one to react. As he reached out and clasped the hands of Sir ji, he asked in a tone dripping with compassion, 'What's the matter, Uncle?'

Choking back his tears with great efforts, Sir ji managed to mumble, 'Son, the memories of this particular time of the year are so painful for this Uncle of yours.'

'Why Uncle? What had happened on this date?'

'It was almost three years ago when I lost my Golu. The cursed date was 5th September 2018.'

Immediately an understanding look came over Ganesh - he recalled Sir ji always carrying the photograph of a youngster, hardly 18-19 years old, in his wallet.

Being a reserved person, he had not asked Sir ji, whose photograph it was, till now. Picking - up courage, he asked softly, 'Uncle, is it his photo that you always carry in your wallet?'

'Yes son, that is my Golu alright' - saying this, Sir ji took out Golu's photo from his wallet and passed it to Ganesh.

'Looks so young!' exclaimed Ganesh as he took the photo and peered at the young, mischievous face looking up at him from the photo. The most arresting feature of that face was a pair of sparkling eyes - they seemed to contain so much promise. Alas! that potential shall always remain unfulfilled now!

'Yes, you are right my boy. Golu, the apple of my eyes, was just 19 when he left us - he was younger than the current age of all of you. He was studying B.Sc in Dyal Singh College in this city - it was his final year. And while he was lovingly called 'Golu' by us, his formal name was equally good: Abhishek.'

'Would you like to share what had happened with Abhishek? If that memory is still too painful, then it's completely okay if you don't.'

'No Ganesh - I do want to share - I do want to talk about my lad - it just brings him alive before my eyes once again. Whenever I close my eyes in bed at night, I can still vividly recall the stark memory of Golu rushing out of our home in a huff after our arguments, and speeding away on his bike on that cursed morning.'

'What was the argument all about?'

'Ah, Ganesh! That memory is so painful! It was an unfortunate father-son argument that we had been having on and off for quite some time. And that was because I had been constantly pressing him to prepare and sit for

Civil Services Examination - my longstanding dream was my only son would become an IAS Officer. But he had radically different ambitions altogether.'

'Right from his childhood, cricket was his passion 24/7 and his vision was to get selected into the national cricket team of India - he constantly dreamt of playing for our country and winning matches for her honour.'

'That's why he used to spend so much more time in the fields honing his cricketing skills rather than in studying the notes of his expensive IAS coaching academy - I had forced him to join there. This was the root of the simmering dispute between the two of us.'

After a while, Sir ji added in a wistful tone, 'Now I so desperately wish that I had never spoken all those harsh words to him. I learnt so late that we must never hurt anyone by words - the pain lingers for such a long time!'

Ganesh nodded his head in complete agreement and then asked in a diffident tone, 'Uncle, would you like to share how did this tragedy happen?'

Sir ji nodded his head in assent and got ready to speak but his tears got better of him.

Ganesh immediately sprang forward and poured him a glass of water from a nearby jug.

After taking a few sips of water and shooting a glance of gratitude toward Ganesh, he resumed in a subdued tone, 'On the morning of that blighted day, as I admitted earlier, we had a bout of our usual IAS vs. Cricket arguments. That made Golu furious and he just stormed out of the house for his college without even waiting to have breakfast. He just got on his bike and shot out of our compound like a rocket.'

'In that year of 2018, a late Monsoon was still active in Delhi - there had been a spell of heavy showers just on the previous evening, due to which the treacherous roads of

Delhi were all slippery.'

'From the eyewitness account of the passersby and Traffic Police, I came to know later on that as his bike took a sharp turn at speed on Lodhi Road, it suddenly lost its balance on the wet surface.'

'As the bike fell, it skidded towards the pavement on the left - but most unfortunately, Golu was thrown towards the right, landing almost bang in the middle of that busy road. And before anyone could do anything, a speeding DTC bus coming from behind mowed him down - it was death on the spot!'

'People around the accident spot did rush him to a nearby hospital. But it was of little use - he had already expired by then. And then around 11 a.m., I received that dreaded phone call from a traffic police constable.'

'From the call log of his mobile phone, which he always carried with him in his shoulder bag while driving, they could trace out my number saved simply as 'Papa' in the mobile address book.'

'Ugh! To see his lifeless body in the mortuary! Never in my worst nightmare did I ever imagine that I would have to face this day in my life...!!'

As the unfortunate father lost his composure in a flood of tears, the four friends in the audience were shocked into a stunned silence.

They could not even begin to fathom the agony of that shattered father in losing his only son in such a ghastly tragedy in the blink of an eye! They desperately tried to hunt for something to say but ultimately decided to remain silent.

After all, the anguish arising out of such inexplicably cruel acts of fate, can't be mitigated by some routine phrases of consolation.

<u>*Points to Ponder:*</u>

- *Death is the inevitable endpoint of every living being: no one has ever escaped its clutches and no one ever will.*
- *So, then, where is the cause to hesitate in giving? Because, at the point of death, everything will be taken away from us in one single instant.*
- *Hence, let each one of us resolve right now to share our wealth of time, money and talent with others, willingly and gladly.*

CHAPTER X

The Greatest Surprise on Earth

<u>*Some words of solace:*</u>
Don't cry because it's over
Smile because it happened.
- Theodore Geisel (Dr Seuss)
The sorrow we feel when we lose a loved one is the price, we pay to have had them in our lives.
- Rob Liano

Sir ji remained immersed in his tearful grief for quite a while. No one spoke and for the moment, the only sound that could be heard was the constant hum of the ceiling fan above, trying its best to dispel the muggy heat of September evening.

Then he visibly took hold of himself and a little later, addressed all the four young men together, 'So guys! As they say, man proposes and God disposes. Like you, my Golu wanted to enjoy his youth to the full - he dreamt of being a cricket champion - he wanted to drive his own car one day - he had ambitions of travelling to exotic locations, - he wished to do so many things.'

'And like an I.T-savvy, fashion-conscious college student of your generation, he was so fond of all his possessions - his beloved cricket bat, his bike, his wardrobe of branded clothes, his costly accessories such as his sunglasses, his iPhone and so on. But alas! Everything was snatched away from him in one single instant on that evil morning three years ago!'

'And in the end, all his dreams, ambitions and desires turned into ashes...! I became the most unfortunate father with the toughest responsibility of consigning the mortal remains of his only son to flames at Nigam Bodh crematorium! So, this life is so very uncertain. One never knows what fate has in store for us next moment.'

'Both I and my wife fell into depression after losing our sole cause of living. Only much later, after receiving spiritual initiation ('Deeksha') at the holy Ramakrishna Mission Ashram at Mandir Marg here in Delhi, we have been able to regain some semblance of composure. But the scars inside us remain green. Most people, I meet, can't detect them under the veneer of my extrovert outer self.'

'Since our initiation through sacred 'Deeksha' a year ago, both of us have made it a habit to go to the holy premises of Ashram every Saturday and Sunday to attend daily evening 'Arati' of Bhagavan Ramakrishna Dev. Thereafter, we stay back for the bi-weekly discourse session of revered Swami Ramananda Ji, the current President of Ashram.'

'And in one such session in June this year, he had talked about the wonderful answer given by Emperor Yudhishthira in response to a question from 'Dharma' (the Divine Entity in Hinduism, responsible for righteousness) in our epic of 'Mahabharat', 'O King, tell me which is the greatest surprise on this earth?' Ganesh, who had been listening intently so far, gave a slight nod for he knew the answer thanks to his Granny's teachings from scriptures and epic.

'Ganesh, it's good that you know the story,' acknowledged Sir ji and continued, 'it is a very famous tale of 'Mahabharat' and the answer given by the emperor will remain eternally valid, 'O Dharma, every single moment men are dying here on this earth. Yet, those who remain alive, think that they will go on living forever - they go about their lives as if they are immortal. This is the greatest surprise on this mortal plane.' It is just so true!'

'After we returned home that evening, I continued to reflect on what I learnt from that session. And I came to realize how fleeting our lives are. Since then, I have yearned to do something good for others in the remaining period of my own life.'

'So, when I overheard Ganesh speak about his meeting the two destitute children at the market-square today morning and his earnest desire to help them somehow, my heart expanded in joy.'

'That's because it just reminded me so much about Golu - one of his brightest virtues was a hidden streak of generosity he had in his heart for everyone in general and stray dogs in particular.'

'Every month, I used to give him a generous amount as a pocket allowance - but instead of spending it entirely on himself, he used to spend a good part of it on buying milk, biscuits etc. every day for his four-legged friends and feed them with his own hands daily evening, after returning from the cricket grounds.'

'Now, I feed them myself after reaching home - they reciprocate with so much love and I feel blessed inside.'

'That's why I felt so appreciative of Ganesh. But then I also could not help overhearing Rakesh as he argued against charity and mocked the good intentions of Ganesh, to boot.'

'That was the point when I decided that I ought not to remain a casual observer on the sidelines any longer. Hence, I resolved to come over to your group to plead with each one of you, in my unfortunate capacity as a first-hand witness to the short duration of this mortal life, to think of others too.'

'This life is so unpredictable. So, I request each one of you, 'Do good. *Have compassion.* Do not ever hesitate in helping others in whatever little way you can. You never know what the next moment may unfold'.'

'As a father, it is my earnest prayer that each one of you should live long. Yet I also need to point out the stark reality - and that reality is that you never know when a rash bus driver will knock your bike down, the way my Golu was so cruelly snatched from me in the prime of his life!'

'So please take a lesson from the misfortune of this heartbroken father, if you can. Given the transitory nature of this life, make charity and benevolence a part and parcel of your life - jump in and live your life to the fullest by serving others - give of your talents fully in the cause of larger humanity. And you will feel blessed in manifold ways.'

'I once more implore each one of you - do your good deed right now - never postpone it for tomorrow - that tomorrow may never come!'

Till now, all the young men had been listening to the emotional entreaties of Sir ji in pin-drop silence. As his soul-stirring plea sank into their hearts, Devesh spoke up in a slow and thoughtful tone, 'You are right, Sir ji. I always keep a quote (credited to Michael Landon Junior) as the wallpaper of my laptop - this says 'Do it, I say. Whatever you want to do, do it now. There are only so many tomorrows!' What you have told us just now tallies exactly with the essence of this profound quote.'

'Yes son, this is what I meant to say,' nodded Sir ji in assent, 'and you have been able to grasp it well. And one last thing I wish to touch upon - please do not take it otherwise, or think that I am needlessly poking into your personal matters. What I am going to say is what I have learnt from my own suffering. And that is the matter of your career choice.'

'As I understand, all of you guys are in the currently fashionable career stream of I.T and in the equally fashionable trend of working for foreign MNCs. But in the deep recess of your heart, one of you may be nursing the dream of doing something completely different.'

'This may be similar to the passionate way in which my Golu always dreamt of playing for the Indian Cricket Team. Now, as a repentant father, I truly appreciate his steadfast adherence to his aspirations despite my constant pressure to give up that uncertain path and instead, choose the conventional career path of Civil Services.'

'If what I am saying makes the slightest sense to you, then my dear boys, I implore you to start heeding the call of your heart at the earliest available opportunity. Because when you do so, then truly honour the specific mission you are meant to accomplish in your individual life - you glorify God who has assigned that mission to you. Then you start finding the true meaning in your life - a sense of such fulfilment allows you to begin thinking and caring for others too.'

'Otherwise, in the soul-crushing rat race you are forced to take part due to relentless pressure of our greedy society, you will be left with no time or even energy, to think of anyone else but yourself. And that is a sure prescription for sustained unhappiness in life.'

'My boys, therefore, give a long and hard look at what you want to do in your life from the above perspective. As it happened in my case, it may even be a matter of life and death - probably, Golu would have been there with me today had I permitted him to freely pursue his dreams and not nagged him constantly to do otherwise.'

'Always keep the catchphrase of 'memento mori' (that I have picked up from revered Swami Ramananda ji) -

remember that you must die - at the back of your mind. We all walk this earth for a very short while indeed.'

'And boys, that brings me to the end of what I wanted to convey to you today. And do pardon me if I have crossed the line and hurt you in any manner during this long monologue of mine.'

Points to Ponder:

- *God is eternal - everything else on this mortal plane is just temporary.*
- *For each one of us, our time remaining on this earth is getting shorter and shorter.*
- *So, let us shake ourselves awake from our false sense of permanence on the earth, and consciously start doing something for the greater good of humanity.*
- *Friends, let us heed the prophetic counsel of Dr A P J Abdul Kalam, 'Let not thy winged days be spent in vain.'*

CHAPTER XI

Let's Do Good Right Now

<u>*Some words of solace:*</u>

You can dance in the storm. Don't wait for the rain to be over before, because it might take too long you can do it now. Wherever you are, right now, you can start ... this very moment.

- Israelmore Ayivor

Yesterday is history;

Tomorrow is a mystery;

Today is God's gift

That's why we call it as the Present.

- Joan Rivers

As Sir ji concluded his impassioned plea, each of his four young participants was found sitting in dazed silence. It was obvious that the emotion-packed punch words had hit their raw nerves and made a mark on their young psyche.

There was pin-drop silence for a long while as they slowly digested the hard-hitting truth of all the emotional outflow that had poured out from the heart of a grieving father.

While all the four men were reeling under the forceful impact of Sir ji's words, probably the greatest churning was going on inside Rakesh. He had just been brought face-to-face with the terrifying reality of the transience of this human life. He discovered that, against his will, it was forcing him to slowly start viewing life from a completely different perspective altogether.

And as he gradually began to realize that all his fellow human beings were on the same train of joy and sorrow as he was, he gave utterance to his feelings in a plaintive voice 'What is the way forward Sir ji? How can I contribute in whatever way I can?'

The way he said it was so different from his usual demeanour of smug self-assurance.

Sir ji took time to consider his thoughts and give a measured reply, 'All of us can be of help to others, in our own ways, my boy.'

'Please tell me how.'

'What I understand from Ganesh is that those two orphan children, Neetu and Sanju need a permanent shelter - 'Ashiana' is at best a stopgap arrangement. So, what one of you guys can do is to go there and meet the In-charge.'

'Then, with his permission, you can meet the children and find out the whereabouts of their other living relatives, if any. Then those relatives can be contacted by us, one by one, to see if they are willing to accept the custody of the children. But I admit the chances of that happening are slim - otherwise, the children would have found a home by now. Anyhow, it's worth a try.'

'In the meanwhile, I shall have a word with revered Swami Ramananda ji to check what is the due process of getting accommodation in a student's home run by Ramakrishna Mission in different cities. And I shall do it right now.'

He was a firm believer in the power of doing good right now, encapsulated so beautifully in a 'Doha' (couplet) of Saint Kabir which says, 'Whatever you have planned for tomorrow, do it today and whatever you want to do today, do it right now'.

Thus, he picked up his mobile immediately and placed a call to the revered Ramananda ji at Ramakrishna Ashram. Since his initiation a year ago, he made it a point to stay in regular touch with the holy company of this pious Monk.

After concluding his call, he announced to the assembled company, 'Revered Maharaj has kindly advised me to meet him tomorrow at Ashram, after the evening 'Arati' of Bhagavan Ramakrishna Dev at Ashram. Let's see what comes out of that meeting.'

'Sir ji, I truly appreciate your promptness,' exclaimed Ganesh, 'you are a true role model for us! Your action loudly demonstrates that any intention for kindness towards others needs to be acted upon immediately.'

'And I am sure that the revered Maharaj, given that he is in the authority of the President of Ashram, will give valuable advice. From my experience of taking part in the humanitarian works of Ramakrishna Mission as a student volunteer, I have come to appreciate the selfless ways in which their Monks serve mankind.'

'Moreover, after chatting with those children, I am sure of one thing.'

'And what's that buddy?' chimed in a curious Devesh.

'I am fairly certain that Neetu and Sanju belong to an educated and decent family - this became clear to me from the innocent but polished way in which they talked to me today, about themselves and their family. I could gather that the girl had been reading in Class IV and the boy in Class II at their school, Saraswati Shishu Mandir back in Meerut.'

'And frankly, I was quite impressed when I found that, unlike run-of-the-mill street beggars who are mostly concerned with getting alms, these children seemed to be much more concerned about resuming their 'padhai' (primary education).'

'Hmm, Ganesh! It seems that they have made quite a favourable impression on you.' commented Sir ji, 'and that brings an idea to my mind. Why don't you bring them over here tomorrow? Five of us plus the two children can have lunch together - it will afford me a good opportunity to meet them and thus, assess them first hand.'

'That's so kind of you, Uncle! I shall pick up my scooty right now and proceed to 'Ashiana' to meet its In-charge and then the children so that the needful can be arranged. And Uncle, when you said you wanted to assess them, could you please share what exactly you have in mind?'

In response to this expected query, Sir ji gave a long sigh and paused for a while. Then he said in a faraway voice, 'Since the time Golu departed, our spacious flat has remained so barren!'

'Three years have now passed since his untimely death, yet it has been so difficult for me as well as my wife to come to terms with that tragedy! It's just so difficult to accept the bitter emptiness in our lives now!'

'So, I was just thinking if Neetu and Sanju could come to our flat and stay with us for a day or two. Tonight, I shall have a word with my wife in this matter and I am sure she would welcome this idea too.'

'I know my wife's nature pretty well. She is genuinely generous at heart and it was clear to me that our son had inherited the same virtue from his mother.'

Sir ji stopped for a moment as he silently re-lived the happy days gone by in the company of his big-hearted son.

'And though it may sound utterly far-fetched right now' he resumed, 'I can even go to the extent of possibly adopting them in future - everything is subject to the approval of my wife, of course.'

'But I know equally well that there will be so many ifs and buts. Unfortunately, adoption as a legal process is still extremely cumbersome in India. It all depends upon the will of Bhagavan Ramakrishna.'

'A magnificent idea!' beamed Ganesh, 'It is truly magnanimous of you to think about those children to this extent! I am simply moved! And I'll make a move to 'Ashiana' now.'

As he got up, Rakesh intercepted him and said, 'Hey Buddy, listen - will you do all the charitable deeds alone? I'll also come with you - we two brothers will do the needful together.'

In reply, Ganesh simply embraced Rakesh, who had the grace to openly admit before everyone, 'Yes buddy! you were right all along...*In our lives, we need to think about others too.*' Then in a soft voice, Ganesh addressed Sir ji, 'Uncle, please grant us the permission to leave now.'

To the smiling nod of Sir ji and joyously approving faces of both Ashok and Devesh, the two friends went out together for their destination, 'Ashiana'.

Points to Ponder:

- *Time and tide wait for none.*
- *With every single out-breath, we are continuously inching closer and closer to our inevitable endpoint of death.*
- *So let us do whatever good we have planned to do right now - the very next moment, we may not be around anymore.*

CHAPTER XII

The Parting Message...

Dear Brothers and Sisters,

Whatever good you have in mind, just go ahead and carry it out right now!

Our transient lives are so full of unexpected twists and turns - one never knows what is going to happen next moment - so, never miss any opportunity to serve others in whatever way you can. Remember, in God's eyes, everything counts.

Always keep in mind that nothing in this mortal plane is permanent. So even if you have been carrying a wound in your heart for a long time, do remember that it is just a temporary phase - better days surely lie ahead of you.

And the surest way to lessen the hurt of your anguish is to contribute, in whatever way you can, towards lessening the pain and tears of others.

Trust in God and move ahead in life. My prayers and best wishes go with you.

May God bless each one of you,

Debanjan

Afterword

Dear Brothers and Sisters,

Now that you've come to the end of this narrative, I sincerely hope that the preceding pages have shown a way how to awaken hope and joy within you.

These pages try to bring out the spiritual message I humbly wished to convey to you.

And to continue to nourish yourself through this spiritual illumination, may I request you to have a glance at some of the profound quotes appended below. These contain the lifetime wisdom of great men over the ages.

As you repeatedly go through these insightful quotes and begin to imbibe their essence, you'll discover that they will directly speak to you and help you to navigate the ups and downs of life with more poise.

Therefore, pick up a quote you like and return to it whenever you are feeling low. Rest assured, as I have discovered many times myself, you will gain a fresh perspective each time you revisit these discerning words.

You will, thus, come to form a virtuous habit of studying spiritually nourishing thoughts that will pay you lifelong dividends. Do remember that such words are extremely potent: they will always guide you toward the right path in life at any given moment.

So, here is a select collection of uplifting thoughts for you:

1. You can't go back and change the beginning but you can start where you are and change the ending. - C S Lewis
2. I choose to make the rest of my life the best of my life. - Louise Hay

3. It is never too late to be what you might have been. - George Eliot

4. Everyone has inside them a piece of good news. The good news is you don't know how great you can be! - Anne Frank

5. And, when you want something, all the universe conspires in helping you achieve it. - Paulo Coelho in 'The Alchemist'

6. Today is where your book begins, the rest is still unwritten. - Natasha Bedingfield in 'Unwritten'

7. Man's main task in life is to give birth to himself to become what he potentially is. - Eric Fromm

8. Start where you are. Use what you have. Do what you can. - Arthur Ashe

9. Remembering that you are going to die is the best way I know to avoid the trap of thinking you have something to lose. You are already naked. There is no reason not to follow your heart. - Steve Jobs

10. Believe you can and you are halfway there. - Theodore Roosevelt

11. We are what we repeatedly do. Excellence, then, is not an act but a habit. - Aristotle

12. The greatest glory in living life lies not in never falling, but in rising every time we fall. - Nelson Mandela

13. The future belongs to those, who believe in the beauty of their dreams. - Eleanor Roosevelt

14. Happiness is not something readymade. It comes from your own actions. - Dalai Lama

15. You have brains in your head. You have feet in your shoes. You can steer yourself in any direction you choose. - Dr Seuss

16. It doesn't matter how slow you go as long as you don't stop. - Confucius

17. Keep your face always toward the sunshine and shadows will fall behind you. - Walt Whitman

18. The only thing that does bring you happiness, is doing something good for somebody, who is incapable of doing it for himself. - David Letterman

19. You don't need to see the whole staircase. Just take the first step. - Martin Luther King Junior

20. God has made all men to be happy. -Epictetus

With these words, I bid you a fond adieu.
May the blessings of God be always with you.
Debanjan

Prayer Of Submission

Dear Maa,

This account is being humbly offered at Your lotus feet as our homage to You.

Please bless us and guide us at every step of our lives.

May the lives of all my readers remain filled with joy and peace.

... This is my prayer to You.

Bowing down to You,

Debanjan

-:Jai Maa:-

9 798888 056189